S____Y

ALBERT MARTIN

A BESTELLERS BOOK

JOHN MURRAY
London

Series director: Robert G. Bander
Designer: Richard Kharibian
Cover designer and illustrator: Warren Lee
Copyright © 1979 by Fearon Pitman Publishers, Inc. This edition
© 1979 by John Murray (Publishers) Ltd.

Printed in the USA
ISBN–0–7195–3695–2

CONTENTS

CHAPTER 1
QUICK-CHANGE ARTIST

Jefferson Avery's vacation was almost over. His visit to his uncle's family in Kenya had ended. So he went to see a travel agent. He wanted to get a plane ticket back to the United States.

The ticket agent gave him a choice. Jeff could fly from Nairobi to Kennedy Airport outside New York City. Or he could fly to Dulles International Airport south of Washington, D.C. The cost was about the same.

Jeff rubbed his ear and thought about it. "I'd like to go to Dulles International Airport," he said. "I've always wanted to visit Washington, D.C. This will give me the chance."

Jeff was given a seat by a window. He was able to look out at a blue morning sky. And the time seemed to fly as fast as the plane. He was given lunch. Then he watched a film. After that he read most of a book. And the next time he looked out, the plane was landing.

Once on the ground, Jeff got his bags. Then he joined one of the lines for the customs check with other people from the plane. He held his cassette recorder in his hand. In his suitcase were tapes of all his favourite records. He took them every time he travelled.

He knew the customs check wouldn't take long. After that he could take a bus into the District of Columbia and see the sights.

Special Agent Thomas Penny looked down through a window at the lines of people going through customs. He was a tall man with black hair and a wide mouth. He looked as if he often smiled, but there was no smile on his face now. "Have you asked your people to hurry?" Penny asked.

Customs Supervisor Alice Bonner, a thin, grey-haired woman, joined Penny at the window. She wore blue police clothes but she carried no gun. She had been in customs work for many years. "Yes, I have. But it will be close. The plane from Rome landed right behind the Nairobi plane."

"We're not interested in the Nairobi plane. It's the one from Rome that's carrying a spy."

"You're sure?" Bonner asked.

"Yes," Agent Penny said. "We have spies of our own."

"But you don't know what name the spy is using?"

"No, we don't. He or she won't be hard to find, though. We know the spy went to school in Canada and speaks English. And he or she will be carrying many tools."

"Tools?" Bonner said.

"Spies have to have equipment," Penny explained. "They have to have things that will help them learn secrets. And once they know secrets, they must have a way to send them home."

Bonner looked surprised. "So all this equipment will come with the spy?"

"Yes," Agent Penny answered.

"But how does the spy think the equipment will get past customs?"

"I'm not sure. But the spy must know that customs people can't open and check every suitcase. It would take far too long."

"You mean he or she hopes that luck will

get the bags through customs without being opened?"

"That's the way it looks," Penny said.

"That doesn't seem very smart," Bonner said. "Maybe the spy has some sure way to get past customs."

"Then we'll have to catch up with the person somewhere else," Penny said. But he wasn't too happy with the thought.

Below, a wave of new people moved across the floor. They joined the passengers already in the lines for the customs check.

"Are those the passengers from the Rome plane?" Penny asked.

"Yes," Bonner answered. "But there are still some people from the Nairobi plane waiting in line."

"Well, I guess that can't be helped. Better get on the telephone and tell your people to be careful. I don't want that spy to get past them," Penny said.

The man called himself George Zack. And he didn't think it was smart to take chances. The only kind of luck he believed in was the kind he made himself. That was why the suitcase that held his equipment was the same as many others on the plane. And his cassette recorder looked the same as one that many people had.

He was not afraid of being caught going through customs. He had switched bags with a woman, leaving his equipment with her. He would go through customs ahead of her and wait. If she got through without trouble, he would go to her. He would explain that a mistake had been made and get back his suitcase. But if she was stopped by customs, he would walk out without saying anything.

That left him with only his cassette recorder to worry about. It was all he had left that could show he was a spy. It looked like a simple recorder, but it wasn't.

Inside, it was different. It could record very, very slowly. Several hours of recording could be put on one short tape. Then, when the tape was played back, it played very fast. And instead of everyone being able to hear it, the sound was sent out over the air by a radio that was hidden within the recorder.

The country he worked for knew when to listen. People from that country were on a ship at sea, waiting to hear from him. All they had to do was record his tape at high speed. When they played it back slowly, they would be able to understand everything.

The recorder was Zack's most important piece of equipment. It was the only way he had of getting in touch with the people he worked for. But he could broadcast for only a minute or two at a time. If he tried to broadcast for a long time, he would be caught. Broadcasting for a short time made it safe for him. But because the recorder played back very fast, he could send long talks. He could send anything he learned out of the country by radio.

George Zack was one of the first people from the Rome plane to reach the customs lines. He got behind Jeff Avery and saw Jeff's cassette recorder. Zack smiled. From the outside, the recorder looked the same as his.

Zack took a map from his pocket. Then he placed his recorder on the floor at his feet. He opened the map and then tapped Jeff on the back. "Can you help me?" he asked, pushing the open map under Jeff's nose. "I'm no good at reading maps."

Jeff put his recorder on the floor so he could hold the map. "Where do you want to go?" Jeff asked.

As they talked, Zack used his foot to push his own recorder forward. Then he used the same foot to pull Jeff's machine to him. A few minutes later it was Jeff who carried the spy's special recorder.

And the line moved closer to the point where the customs check would be made.

CHAPTER **2**

WRONG SUITCASE

The line Jeff stood in had slowed down. Jeff looked at the other lines. They, too, were going more slowly than before. It seemed that the customs people had decided to give everything a close look. And that had started when the people from the Rome plane had joined the lines.

I'll bet they think someone is going to try to slip something into the country, Jeff thought. He held his recorder against his side. When the line moved forward, he did, too.

After a while, it was Jeff's turn at customs.

"Passport, please," the customs agent said. The name Miller was above the pocket of the man's coat.

Jeff handed him a thin, blue book with gold letters on its cover.

Miller looked at Jeff's picture in the book, then at Jeff. "This says you're from Chicago. Is that where you're going, Mr. Avery?"

"Yes," Jeff answered.

"Why did you come this way? There are more planes going to Chicago from New York. You would have had a better choice of planes."

"I'm on vacation," Jeff explained. "And I've never seen Washington. I thought I'd stop here for a few days on my way home."

"I see," Miller said. He returned the passport to Jeff. "Please open your suitcases," he said.

Jeff had only two. He opened them on the table in front of the agent.

The agent picked up a yardstick. As he went through the bags, he used the yardstick to check them, too. He made sure the inside of each bag was almost as big as the outside. If there were any secret places to hide things, he would find them. But there weren't any. The bags held only clothes and some presents for Jeff's parents.

Jeff wasn't trying to hide the recorder he carried. He didn't think he had to hide it. But Miller didn't even look at it. "Enjoy your stay in Washington," he said, and let Jeff close his bags. The inspection was over.

George Zack had been standing next to Jeff Avery. He had been able to see and hear everything. Now he stood and watched the young man slip from sight into the crowd.

"Papers, please," Miller said, forcing Zack to turn around.

Zack brought a thin, blue book from his pocket. He handed it to the customs agent.

Miller looked at the picture in the book and then at Zack. "You were born in Oklahoma City?" he said.

"Yes," Zack answered. "But I've lived in and around Washington for the last ten years."

Miller handed back Zack's passport. "Please open your bags," he said.

Like Jeff, Zack had two suitcases. He put them on the table and opened one. It was stuffed with his clothes.

The customs agent began to go through it, checking its size with his yardstick. Everything was all right. "The other bag, please," the agent said. "It must be opened too."

Zack took a small key from his pocket. It was the key to his own bag. With luck it would also open this bag—the one he had taken from the woman. He put the key into the lock and gave it a turn. But it didn't work.

"What's the matter?" Miller asked.

"Er—ah—my key doesn't work," Zack said.

"Are you sure it's the right key?"

"I thought it was. . . ."

"But now you're not sure?"

Zack gave a weak smile.

The customs agent reached down. He brought up a ring of keys from his side of the table. He picked one and tried it. It didn't work, so he tried another. The second key opened the bag.

The bag was full of clothes. But they belonged to a woman, not a man. The agent gave Zack a questioning look.

"They belong to my wife," Zack said, thinking fast.

"Oh?" Miller said. The only people near Zack were men. "And where is she?"

"She'll be on the next plane," Zack said. His mind was racing.

"The next plane?"

"Yes," Zack explained. "We never fly to-gether. We have children at home, and she's afraid of a crash. This way, if there is a crash, there will always be one of us to care for the kids."

"A lot of married people feel that way," the customs agent said. He started to push the bags away, then stopped. "Let me have another look at that suitcase," he said.

CHAPTER 3
THE ABC

Bonner, the customs supervisor, turned from the window that looked down on the customs lines. Even before she spoke, Agent Penny knew something had happened. Bonner's face said it all. Something had turned up.

"They found something! Line three. Let's get down there," Bonner said. She led the way to the customs lines at a run.

When they reached line three, they found a group of customs agents. They were questioning a woman who was dressed in a beautiful brown and white suit. She wore sunglasses with large frames. On the customs table was an open suitcase. It held cameras, guns, tools for opening safes and locks, and many other things.

"You didn't say the spy was going to be a woman," Bonner said.

"I didn't know," Special Agent Penny answered. "It's a surprise to me, too."

"She doesn't look like my idea of a spy," the customs supervisor said.

"What does a spy look like?" Penny asked.

"I don't know," Bonner said. "But it can't be like that. She acts like the head of some company or other."

The woman in line three shook her head and pointed at the open bag. "That isn't mine," she said. "I don't own those things."

Penny walked over to her. "You were asked to place your bags on the table, weren't you?" he asked.

"Of course."

"And this is one of the bags you put there, isn't it?"

"Yes. It looks just like mine. But, believe me, it isn't."

Agent Penny and Supervisor Bonner took a step back so they could talk without others hearing. "I think you're right," Penny told Bonner. "If she's a spy, she's in the wrong business. She could win an Academy Award."

"It should be simple to tell if she's the spy," Bonner said.

"It should?"

"Uh-huh. Let me talk to her," Bonner said.

Bonner went to the woman. "You seem to be a woman who knows her ABC," she said.

"It's kind of you to say so," said the woman. "I think I do."

Bonner broke in. "Well, then, tell me the last three letters," she said.

The woman looked at Bonner for a few seconds. Then she said, "*Ex, why,* and *zee,*"

Bonner thanked the woman and went back to Penny. "That proves it," Bonner said. "She's not the spy."

Now it was Penny's turn to shake his head. "How can you be sure? Don't you think spies learn the ABC?"

"A lot of people come into this country every year," Bonner said. "Some of them try to make us think they were born here when they weren't."

"So?"

"So," Bonner went on, "customs had to find ways to trip them up."

"And that's where the ABC comes in?"

"Right. You said the spy had gone to school in Canada, didn't you?"

"Yes."

"Well," Bonner said, "they don't say *ex, why,* and *zee* in Canada."

Penny was surprised. "They don't? What do they say?"

"*Ex, why,* and *zed,*" Bonner told him. "That's

the British way. And that's the way they teach the ABC in Canada."

"I didn't know that," Penny said.

"Now you do," Bonner said, smiling.

They moved back to the woman.

"It looks like someone switched bags with you," Bonner told her. "We'll follow it up."

"Yes," Penny put in. "That's what must have happened." Then he drew Bonner aside and said, "The spy is probably long gone by now. He or she wouldn't have gone through customs behind the woman, only ahead of her. That way the person could get away if your customs people opened the bag."

"And return her bag if we didn't," Bonner finished for him.

Miller was one of the customs agents standing around Bonner and Penny. He left the group and stopped in front of Customs Supervisor Bonner. "Ms. Bonner," he said.

"Yes, what is it?"

"A man came through my line a few minutes ago. He had two bags. One was like that one. It was full of women's clothes."

"And what did you do?" Penny asked before Bonner could say anything.

"I checked it out," Miller said. "He said the clothes belonged to his wife." Miller made a face. "I had an idea something was wrong. I just couldn't put my finger on it."

"But you still let him walk away?" Bonner asked.

Miller said, in a weak voice, "I went through his bags a second time. That's all I could do."

"Well, maybe everything isn't lost. Do you know what name he is going by?" Bonner asked.

"Yes. He was the first man I checked from the Rome plane. I remember that. His name is George Zack. His papers looked OK."

"I'm sure they did," Penny said. "And I'm just as sure they weren't. He probably has a new name already."

Penny seemed to think for a few seconds. He looked at the open bag and its spy equipment without speaking. Then he said, "Miller, did that man have anything with him besides his suitcases?"

"Yes. He had a cassette recorder. How did you know?"

"Just a guess. That piece of spy equipment is not in this bag. Did you check the recorder?"

"I sure did. That was the last thing I looked at. In fact, I almost missed it. I had to call him back. I opened it up, then played part of the tape that was in it."

"What was on the tape?"

"Music. Hard rock."

Penny turned to Bonner. "I'm going to need a list of everyone who has already passed through customs. From the Rome plane, that is. Better give me the names of the last few people in line from the Nairobi plane, too."

"That's going to be a lot of work," Bonner said.

"But it will be worth it," Penny told her. "Unless I'm wrong, one of those people has a very good chance of ending up dead. Once I have that list, your job is over. Then it will be up to me. I'll have to find out who's in trouble and help."

"Aren't you even going to tell me what is going on?"

"No," Penny said.

"That's not fair," Bonner said. "I told you about the ABC."

"Who told you life is fair?" Penny said.

CHAPTER **4**

WHERE'S THE SPY?

The spy had thought he would never get past customs. The customs agent had gone through his bags twice. Then, as Zack was walking away, he had been called back. Miller had decided to check the recorder, too.

It was a good thing he had switched recorders the same way he had changed bags. If he hadn't, he would have had to face a lot of questions. Questions he didn't want to answer.

He put the bags down and waited. He was standing where he could see the woman who had his equipment bag. She was getting close to the customs agent, and it didn't look as if she would get past him. Every agent was making everyone open every bag.

They weren't this careful all the time. The spy was sure they weren't. That told him they were looking for something. Or someone. And if it was someone, that someone was probably him.

It was very warm in the airport, but the spy felt cold. It was as though a piece of ice was being held against his back.

He pretended he was mending the handle of the recorder. All the while he watched the woman move towards the customs agent.

When a customs agent pointed to the equipment bag, the spy started moving again. Even if they didn't know about him already, they soon would. He had to put some miles between himself and the airport.

And he had to get his recorder back.

But first things first. He ducked into a men's room where he could be by himself. He took everything out of his pockets with the name George Zack on it. He threw away all those papers and cards.

Then he opened the bag that held his clothes. He found a light blue sports coat. In one of its pockets was another set of papers, one that used the name William Jones. He took off the coat he wore and put on the sports coat.

When he walked out of the men's room, he left the woman's bag behind. Now all he carried were his clothes and Jeff Avery's cassette recorder. Now he was safe.

He was sure he could catch up with the man who had his recorder. He had heard the customs man call him "Mr. Avery." And he had seen the letters "J.A." on his bags. So the man who had his recorder was named J. Avery.

The spy also knew that J. Avery planned to stay in Washington a few days. That's what he had told the customs agent. If he was going to stay with friends, he probably would have said that, too. That meant J. Avery would be checking into a hotel.

The man who now called himself William Jones took a bus to Washington, D.C. When he got there, he bought $5 worth of change. Then he found a telephone and began calling the hotels.

"Has Mr. J. Avery checked in, yet?" he asked.

When he called the Hotel Hartford, he was told, "Yes, sir. Shall I ring his room?"

"No, thank you," Jones said. "I just wanted to be sure he got there OK."

Jones hung up the phone and looked at his map of Washington, D.C. The Hotel Hartford was only three blocks from where he was. He gave a pleased smile. Then he picked up his bag and the recorder and started walking towards the Hartford.

Special Agent Thomas Penny waited until Bonner, the customs supervisor, gave him the list of names. Then he didn't waste any more time at the airport. He hurried to his office in Washington. There he told Inspector Sullivan what had happened.

"The spy got past customs, sir," Penny said. "The woman's suitcase was found in a men's room just before I left for here."

"*Now* what are you going to do?" Inspector Sullivan wanted to know.

"We'd better watch our step. The spy *must* know we're on his trail. If he gets his equipment back, he'll probably kill the person who had it. That would be the smart thing for the spy to do. If the person is dead, he or she can't tell us anything about the spy."

Inspector Sullivan pressed his mouth into a thin, hard line. "Then you'd better get that machine before the spy does. Take all the agents you need."

CHAPTER 5
A BROKEN RECORDER

Jeff washed and changed into clean clothes. Then he decided to listen to some music. He pushed the play button to turn on the cassette machine.

Nothing seemed to happen.

What's wrong? he wondered. Don't tell me it's broken already.

He picked up the recorder and looked at the cassette. It had run out. He took it out, turned it over, and put it back. Again he pushed the play button, but it didn't make a sound.

Jeff leaned down to get a better look. The tape was turning. It was turning fast! He had never seen it go so fast. And not a sound was coming from the machine.

Jeff had bought his cassette recorder a week before he went to Nairobi. He had been afraid he might have trouble taking it past customs. To be safe he had brought his receipt and his other papers with him.

Now he went to his bag and got out the papers. There was a list of places across the country that were able to mend the machine. He checked if any of them was in Washington.

He was in luck. There was a place on 16th Street. The Hotel Hartford was on 10th Street, so it was close enough for him to walk.

He took the elevator down to the hotel lobby. The Hartford was on the corner of 10th and F Streets. The hotel had doors leading to both streets. He left through the 10th Street door.

A minute later, William Jones came into the hotel from the F Street side. He stopped inside the door, looked around the lobby, then went to the desk.

"I'd like a room," Jones told the clerk.

"Yes, sir. How long will you be staying with us?"

"A day or two," Jones said.

"I'm sure you'll enjoy your stay here," the clerk said. He gave a white card to Jones. "Fill this in, please."

Jones wrote down a lot of new lies. He said his name was Walter Marlowe and that he was from Cleveland.

"By the way," Jones said, handing back the card, "I have a friend staying here—Mr. Avery. Could I have a room on his floor?"

The clerk looked into a card box, then said, "Yes, sir. We have a nice room on the third floor. I'll get someone to show you the way and help you with your bag. You'll be in 314. Mr. Avery is around the corner in 320." He rang a bell on the desk. "Front!" he called.

A young man took the room key from the clerk. The two men walked to the elevator.

Jeff Avery had found the shop that mended recorders. But it was not as close as he had thought. After reaching 16th Street, he had had to walk north on 16th another nine blocks.

The woman in the shop could not mend the recorder straight away. She didn't even have time to look at it now.

"Here," she said. She gave Jeff an orange ticket. "Come back in a day or so. If it's something simple, I'll have it fixed by then. If it isn't, I'll tell you what's wrong. Fair enough?"

Jeff put the orange ticket into the pocket of his shirt. "OK," he said. "Fair enough."

The spy inched open the door of his room and looked out. No one was in the corridor. He stepped outside and pushed the door closed behind him.

He went into the corridor, keeping near the wall. He knew the floor near the wall wouldn't make sounds as he passed.

His room, 314, was in the east wing. Room 320 was in the south wing. He turned the corner and stopped outside Avery's room. Then he pressed his ear to the door. Not a sound. Either

Avery had gone out or he was in a deep sleep.

If the spy's equipment was in the room, this might be the right time to get it. But he had no way of getting into the room. He said something angrily to himself and turned away.

He left the hotel and walked along F Street. As he went, he looked into shop windows. Soon he found what he was looking for. He went inside.

"That's sharp enough to cut hair," the clerk in the shop said. He showed Jones a long knife.

"Good," Jones said. "I'll take it."

He returned to the hotel and took a seat in the lobby. He pretended that he was reading a paper, and waited.

If Avery was out, he would stop at the desk for his key when he came back. Then he would go to the third floor.

But if he was in his room sleeping, there would be no problem. If Avery didn't show up in the lobby soon, the spy would know he must be in his room.

The spy didn't want to telephone the room or ask for Avery. If Avery was sleeping, he wanted him to stay that way.

Also, he didn't know what he might have to

do before he got his recorder back. If he asked for Avery, he might be remembered. He didn't want to be remembered. He had already made the mistake of saying he was Avery's friend.

Jones didn't see Avery come into the hotel from 10th Street. But he did see him cross the lobby and go to the desk for his room key. With the key in his hand, he turned and walked to the elevator.

The man with many names got slowly to his feet. He crossed the lobby and took the next car up to the third floor.

CHAPTER **6**

THIEF IN THE NIGHT

Special Agent Penny had been given 25 men and women to help him. He met them outside the telephone rooms near his office. In the hours ahead, he was sure the telephone would be their most important tool.

"There are 163 people, both men and women, we must find," Penny told them. "When we do, they have to be asked a few questions:

"One, were they carrying a cassette recorder when they got off the plane at Dulles International Airport?

"Two, if so, does it now work as it should?

"Three, did it perhaps get mixed up with someone else's recorder and not get back to them until they had passed customs?"

Penny smiled like a man who is sure of himself. But he wasn't. "Each of you will be given six or more names. The passport office has already given us the people's home telephone numbers. Call there first. If they aren't home, try to find out where they are."

The names and telephone numbers were handed out. "OK," Penny said. "Get cracking!"

The spy waited until he saw no light under Jeff's door. Then, to be on the safe side, he waited an hour more.

Finally, he pressed his ear to the door and listened. He didn't want to make a mistake. Just because the light was out didn't mean Jeff was sleeping. He could be watching TV.

There was no sound. So he *was* sleeping. Good.

The man with many names took the knife from his pocket. He slid it into the crack of the door. In a few seconds, he had the door open. It was so fast he couldn't have done it more easily with a key.

He stepped inside and closed the door behind him. The room was dark. He stayed where he was until his eyes got used to it. Then he moved forward without a sound.

The light from a full moon was coming through the window. He could see Jeff on the bed. He was on his back. His chest was going up and down slowly.

The spy looked around the room. He spotted Jeff's suitcases and went to them. One at a time, he opened them and felt inside.

There was nothing that was the right size or shape to be a cassette recorder.

Where could it be?

There was a chest of drawers against the far wall. He went to it and looked inside each drawer. Again, nothing.

What was left? He looked around the room one more time. Beside the bed was a low table. It had a drawer that might be big enough to hold the recorder.

He moved back to the bed. As he reached out a hand to open the drawer, he looked down at Jeff.

And he found that Jeff was looking up at him.

Special Agent Penny called his people together again. They had been able to reach all but 16 of the plane passengers.

"You've done a great job so far," Penny told them. "But time is running out. The longer it takes us to find the right person, the more chance there is that the spy can get to him or her first. Remember, the spy probably knows where to look. If he didn't think he could find the person again, the switch wouldn't have been made."

"That sounds right," someone said, and other voices said the same thing.

"OK, stop talking and start listening," Penny said. "Some of you have finished all your calls. I want you to help those who still have passengers to find. I know you're checking to see if they left Washington by air for other cities. I know you're checking hotels in other parts of the country. And I know the job doesn't get any easier. But it has to be done. I'll buy lunch all week for the person who finds the passenger we're looking for."

"What will you be doing while we wear out the telephones?" someone wanted to know.

"Worrying," Penny said.

The spy stopped moving when he saw that

Jeff's eyes were open. He had been told this sometimes happened. A person's eyes might open if he was dreaming.

It isn't anything to worry about by itself, he thought to himself. Chances are he doesn't see anything.

The spy was telling himself these things when Jeff sat up suddenly. He caught the spy's arm as he tried to get away. Then Jeff pulled him to the floor.

"Who are you?" Jeff asked. "What do you want?"

The spy tried to pull away, but Jeff's hold became more strong. William Jones put his foot against the bed and pushed.

Jeff let go suddenly, and the spy went flying across the room. He crashed into the chest of drawers and fell to the floor. The wind had been knocked out of him.

Jeff threw himself at the spy. The two men rolled around on the floor like angry children. But they hit each other with strong blows.

Jones had dropped his knife when the fight started. He had been taken by surprise. Now he tried to hold Jeff back and hunt for the knife at the same time. At last, he got hold of the knife. But he cut himself as he did.

Jones brought his arm round with all the power he had. The heavy handle of the knife hit the side of Jeff's head with the force of a thrown rock. Still Jeff tried to hang on, but his hold became weak. His fingers opened, and the spy slipped free.

Jones headed for the door as fast as he could. Once outside the room, he turned and raced down the hall. He was hoping he could get back to his own room before Jeff called for help.

But Jeff didn't call for help. The blow on his head had dazed him—but he came to fast. What he did was far better for him than calling for help. Jeff screamed, "Fire!" People who might have pretended they didn't hear a cry for help ran to their doors.

The spy was almost in his own room when the door across the hall opened. A woman's head came out, and William Jones kept going. He turned his face away as he ran down the hall.

He couldn't go into his room while the woman was watching. He only hoped the woman had not seen him before and didn't know where his room was.

After he was well past the woman, Jones looked back. The woman was looking at him with her mouth hanging open.

Then Jones saw he still held the knife in his hand. And it was covered with blood.

CHAPTER **7**
ON THE RUN

When he felt strong enough, Jeff got to his feet. He knew the man was gone. He didn't try to follow him. Instead, he picked up the telephone and called the hotel desk.

"This is Mr. Avery in room 320," he said. "I just woke up and found a man in my room."

"Are you sure?" the desk clerk asked.

"That's not a very smart question," Jeff said. "Yes, I *am* sure. If you don't believe me, come up and look at the marks on me."

"You mean you're hurt?"

"He hit me with something, but I'll live." Jeff touched his head. "Maybe."

Jeff had hardly hung up the telephone before the desk clerk knocked at his door.

"Come in!" Jeff called from the bed. Just then, the bed felt very good to him.

The clerk came in with two police officers.

Jeff told them what had happened, and the police started to look around the room.

One officer had red hair and a slow way of talking. Her name was Ruth Bainbridge. She seemed to do everything slowly. But she didn't seem lazy. It was as if she was being careful to get things right the first time.

The other was young and new to the job. His name was Mike Wyman. He seemed to be in a hurry. Too much of a hurry to get anything right the first time.

"Hey, look at this!" Wyman called. "There's blood over there." He pointed to a spot near the chest of drawers. "And the drops lead out into the corridor."

Bainbridge came over to look. She leaned down and touched one of the spots of blood. It was wet. "That's fresh blood, all right."

"Say, we can follow that trail straight to the man," Wyman said. "Come on!" Without waiting for his partner, he ran from the room. He was taking his gun out as he went.

Bainbridge looked at Jeff and shook her head. "I'm supposed to be breaking him in on the job," she said. "I had better catch up with him before he follows those drops of blood into the

street. He'd be hit by a lorry for sure." She walked from the room and turned the same way Mike had.

Jeff watched her go. Then he got slowly to his feet. He hurt all over. One of his eyes hurt and it would probably swell up badly. And his mouth had come out second best when the spy's head had crashed into it.

Jeff went to the door and closed it.

His vacation had been great until now. He wondered if things could get worse.

The spy pushed open the door to the fire stairs and started to climb. When he came to the tenth floor, he ran down the corridor past the elevator to the stairs to the roof. He didn't stop running until he was on top of the hotel.

He felt safe there. No one had seen him except that one woman. And she hadn't had a very good look.

Now he had to do something about his hand. He had cut two of his fingers with his own knife. Running down the corridor with it still in his hand, he must have looked like a madman. Both the knife and his hand were covered with blood.

He pulled out his shirt and cut a piece from the bottom. He put that around his fingers and tied the ends. That stopped the blood.

The blood! He had been leaving a trail of blood!

If the police had been called, they were probably following it right now. He looked around to see if there was a place for him to hide.

There wasn't.

He had to get off the roof. Now that the blood had been stopped, he had to get away from the trail that led to him.

He stepped towards the stairs, but he was met by Wyman who came out on to the roof.

"Hold it right there, mister!" Wyman called.

"Who, me?" the spy asked with wide eyes.

Wyman had not been on the force long. He didn't know that he had to be most careful of men with wide eyes who said, "Who, me?"

And men who came walking towards him as the spy did now, looking as if he was on his way to tea.

Wyman started to step back, but he was too late. The spy kicked the gun out of his hand.

In the next minute and a half, the spy was all over him like water on a fish. When the fight was over, the spy had Wyman's gun. And Mike was out cold. When he came to, he would find he had a cut mouth and a broken arm. But for now he could feel nothing.

Jones put the gun under his coat. And he put his hurt hand into his pocket. When he went down the steps from the roof, he looked like a man without a care in the world.

He had to wait for the elevator on the tenth floor. He was still there when Bainbridge went past, following the trail of blood.

The Hotel Hartford was an old hotel. Its elevator was slow. Jones thought it would never get to the tenth floor. Then, just as the two police officers came from the roof, one helping the other, the door opened.

Jones stepped into the car, but not before Wyman saw him. "There he is!" he shouted. "That's the man!"

The police officers ran towards the elevator. Jones gave the elevator door an angry kick, and it closed. Then the car started to drop slowly towards the lobby.

Jones was sure that Bainbridge and Wyman could run down the stairs and get to the lobby first. It seemed very warm inside the car. Then the elevator stopped at the fifth floor. Three more people got on. When it started moving again, it seemed to move even more slowly. And Jones's shirt was sticking to his back.

Finally, after what seemed like hours, the elevator door opened in the lobby. The other people got off ahead of Jones. Then he could see there were two more police officers at the desk. One was talking on the telephone.

As Jones watched, the officer put the telephone down. Then he made a quick turn towards the elevator. It was clear the officers up above had called on a hotel telephone. The police from the desk were coming towards him.

Again the spy pushed an elevator button. The door closed before the police could reach for him.

Wyman held his broken arm close to his side. He and his partner were walking by the elevator door on the second floor, on their way down from the tenth floor.

"The elevator is coming up," he said. He could hear the sound of its motor.

"Well, push the button," Bainbridge said. "Make it stop here so we can ride the rest of the way down."

When the car reached the second floor, the door opened. The police officers got into the empty car and rode down to the lobby. There, the door opened again, and Wyman and Bainbridge faced the other police.

"What happened?" one of the new officers asked. "The man you wanted us to stop didn't get off the elevator. He went back up in it. It stopped only once, then came down with you two. How did he get past you?"

"There wasn't anyone in the car when it got to the second floor," Bainbridge said. "It was empty."

"Then where did he go?" they asked each other. "Where *could* he have gone?"

But no one had an answer.

CHAPTER **8**

A Friend in Room 314

Special Agent Penny told Inspector Sullivan where the hunt now stood. "We have it down to three people," he said. "Two of them were on the Rome plane. The other one was on the plane from Nairobi."

"Do you have any idea of where to look for them?"

"No. We called their homes, and that didn't help. No one knew what their plans were."

"Where does that leave us?" Sullivan asked.

"I have my people making more telephone calls. That's all I can do. Some are calling ticket agents to see if any of the passengers is on a plane for another city. Others are calling hotels around here to see if they have checked in."

"Too bad you can't cut this short in some way."

"I'm doing my best," Penny said. "The spy probably switched bags with someone from the

Rome plane. So I have everyone working on those two names. I think we can save the Nairobi passenger, a man named Avery, for last."

When Jeff woke up, the sky was turning pink. It was almost light. Jeff decided to go out and get something for his aching head.

The same desk clerk was working. Because the police were there, he hadn't gone home. Jeff dropped his key on the desk and started to leave.

"Mr. Avery?" the clerk said.

"Yes?"

"I'm really sorry about what happened. That kind of thing *never* happens at the Hartford."

"It did this time," Jeff said.

"Yes, yes it did. It's too bad your friend wasn't with you. I'm sure the two of you could have taken care of one thief."

"My friend?" Jeff asked. "What do you mean?"

"Your friend. The man who wanted to be on the same floor with you. Mr. Marlowe in room 314."

"Oh, *that* friend," Jeff said, as he took back his key. "I'll go and have a talk with him."

CHAPTER 9
FACE TO FACE

The spy hadn't been able to sleep. He had been too nervous to sleep. Once he got back to his room, the sounds made by the police in the corridor kept him awake.

To help pass the time, he began to change his looks. He parted his hair in a different way. That helped a little. Then he put paper into his mouth to change the shape of his face. That was a little better.

The cuts on his fingers were not as bad as he had thought. He had washed and cleaned them. Now they were covered by only a thin strip taken from a white shirt.

That business with the elevator had been very close. When he thought of how close, he had to shake his head in wonder. The elevator car had slowed down to stop at the second floor. Somehow he had known the police were there.

He had looked around for a way to escape. That was when he saw the small door up in the roof of the car. In a flash, he had jumped up and pulled himself through the opening.

Then, when the police were getting into the car below him, he had used his knife to force open the door on the third floor. Luck was with him. There was no one in the corridor. He was able to get to his room without being seen.

After that, he had felt better. He had control of things again. The police had come to his room, asking if he had seen or heard anything.

He had been able to lie like the trained spy he was. They had smiled and gone away.

Suddenly, there was a knock at the door. Was it the police again? It was possible.

He opened the door. But he kept one hand on the gun he had taken from the young police officer. There in front of him stood Jeff Avery.

"You!" Avery said. It was clear from his face that he remembered the spy from their talk at the airport, even with his changed looks. "It was you in my room last night!" It wasn't a question.

The spy pointed the gun at him. "And it is you in my room this morning," he said, with a pleased smile. "Step right this way, or you'll be very sorry for the last few seconds you live."

Jeff looked ill. "You've got a police gun," he said, doing as he was told.

"Too bad for you," Jones said, closing the door behind him. "Now you can tell me what you did with my cassette recorder."

"Your recorder? I don't know what you're talking about."

"I switched recorders with you at the airport. You carried mine through customs, and I carried yours."

"And now you want yours back. That's why you were in my room last night."

"You catch on fast," Jones told him.

"Well, I have some news for you. I don't have your recorder now. I—I lost it," Jeff said.

"If you can't get me my recorder," Jones said, "I don't need you." He pointed the gun at Jeff's head. "I'm going to give you until I count to three. If you don't tell me where my recorder is, I'm going to blow a hole in you. One, two . . .," he began.

"OK, you win," Jeff said.

"I thought I would," Jones told him.

Special Agent Penny had been awake all night. Now he was drinking a cup of strong coffee to help him stay that way. He was in a small room. It didn't have much more space than was needed for the coffee pot, a table, and a few chairs. A radio was broadcasting the morning news.

Penny was looking into his coffee cup, almost too tired to listen. Then he heard the name Jefferson Avery. He turned up the radio and forgot about his coffee.

A few minutes later he rushed to where the

other agents were busy on the telephones.
"Never mind those two men from the Rome
plane," he said. "Jefferson Avery is the man we
want. And he's right here in town."

Penny pointed a finger at a few of his agents
"You, you, and you—come with me," he said.
"The rest of you might as well go home and get
some sleep."

Penny and his agents parked on 10th Street.
Then they ran to the hotel desk. The police
had left the hotel long before, thinking the
thief had got away.

"Is Mr. Avery in his room?" Penny asked.

The clerk didn't have to look to see if Jeff's
key was in its box. He knew the answer without
looking. "No, sir. He left a few minutes ago with
a friend."

CHAPTER **10**

THE RIGHT ANSWER

Jeff walked ahead of the spy all the way to the shop where he had left the recorder. It was closed.

"Is this some kind of trick?" Jones cried, his eyes giving off angry flashes.

"No, no," Jeff said in a hurry. "It's just too early. They open in two hours. See the sign?"

Jones looked at the sign in the window. "Oh, yeah. OK. But I don't want to wait that long."

"What's so important about that recorder? It doesn't even work," Jeff said.

"Never mind why I want it. Just remember what's going to happen to you if I don't get it," Jones said. "Walk around to the back. Maybe we can get inside that way."

"Look through their rooms," Penny told his agents. "They weren't carrying anything when they left here. You'll probably find one of the recorders in room 314."

In a few minutes his agents were back with a recorder. "Does it work?" Penny asked.

"Yes, sir."

"That's what I was afraid of," Penny said. "The only reason they could have for leaving here together is to get the spy's machine."

"What could Avery have done with it?" one of Penny's agents asked.

"What do you men think?" Penny asked, and got blank looks in return. "What would you do with a recorder if it wasn't working?"

"Take it back to the place where I bought it," one of the agents said.

"And if you were away from home?" Penny pressed.

"I'd get it mended somewhere else."

"Right," Penny said. "Now, check the telephone book. See if there is anyone around here who mends this kind of recorder."

Jones found his machine in the back room of the shop. He checked it over slowly. He was careful to see it was as it should be. But to check the machine, he had to take his eyes off Jeff.

He shouldn't have.

Jeff picked up one of the heavy shop tools and brought it down on Jones's arm. Jones dropped the gun, and Jeff had it in his hand before it could hit the floor.

"Now it's my turn to give orders," Jeff said, jumping away from him.

"I don't take orders," Jones said. He wore an ugly smile. Slowly he pulled his knife from his pocket. "Have you ever shot anyone?" he asked.

"No," Jeff said.

"It's not as easy as you may think." He took a step towards Jeff.

"Maybe not," Jeff said. "But if you come any closer I'm going to shoot."

The two men stood, looking at each other over a space of six feet.

"Everything has gone wrong for me," Jones said. "And it's all because of you. You're bad luck."

"Don't move," Jeff told him.

"I'm going to kill you if it's the last thing I do," Jones said.

Suddenly Penny was at the broken window Jeff and Jones had used to get into the shop.

"All right, don't move you two!" Penny called. "You with the gun—drop it."

"I—I can't," Jeff called back.

"Drop it!" Penny ordered a second time. "I won't tell you again."

"He has a knife," Jeff explained. "He'll kill me if I drop the gun."

"No, I won't," Jones lied. "Shoot him. He's the man you want." As he spoke, he got ready to throw himself at Jeff as soon as the gun fell.

"You with the gun," Penny called again. "What are the last three letters of the ABC?"

"*Ex, why,* and *zee,*" Jeff answered.

"That's right," Penny called back. Then he put his gun away and took his time climbing through the window.

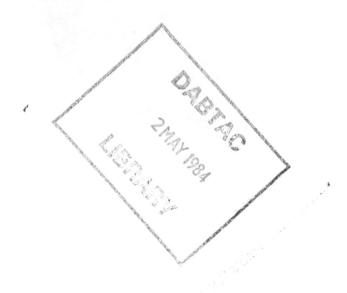